Whitney
the Whale
Fairy

by Daisy Meadows

Join the Rainbow Magic Reading Challenge!

Read the story and collect your fairy points to climb the
Reading Rainbow at the back of the book.

This book is worth 5 points.

The Fairyland Palace

GALA
FAIRYLAND ROYAL AQUARIUM

Fairyland Royal Aquarium

Kirsty's Gran's House

Lighthouse

The Park

Rockpool

Ocean Star Sailing Ship

Lea-On-Sea

Whales

The Magical Conch Shell at my side,
I'll rule the oceans far and wide!
But my foolish goblins have shattered the shell,
So now I cast my icy spell.

Seven shell fragments, be gone, I say,
To the human world to hide away,
Now the shell is gone, it's plain to see,
The oceans will never have harmony!

Contents

All Aboard the Ocean Star

"This is brilliant fun, Kirsty!" Rachel
Walker called to her best friend, Kirsty
Tate, as their ship, the *Ocean Star*, bobbed
across the waves. "Look, can you see that
shoal of fish?"

Kirsty peered over the ship's rail and
saw the tiny, silvery fish darting through
the sparkling turquoise water. Some of
the other girls and boys on the boat trip
rushed over to look, too.

"Leamouth looks so lovely in the sunshine, doesn't it?" Kirsty remarked, as they sailed across the bay. She and Rachel stood on the deck of the *Ocean Star*, enjoying the view of the pretty seaside resort with its golden beach and whitewashed cottages clustered around the harbour.

Kirsty and Rachel were spending the spring holiday in Leamouth with Kirsty's gran. Gran had suggested that today the girls took a special trip just for children on an old-fashioned sailing ship, run by Captain Andy and his crew.

Rachel and Kirsty were fascinated by the large wooden boat with its tall masts and huge, billowing white sails.

"Ahoy there, sailors!" Captain Andy shouted, waving at the girls and boys on the deck below him. He was standing behind the wooden ship's 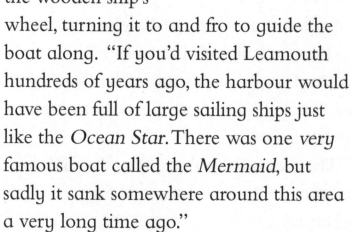 wheel, turning it to and fro to guide the boat along. "If you'd visited Leamouth hundreds of years ago, the harbour would have been full of large sailing ships just like the *Ocean Star*. There was one *very* famous boat called the *Mermaid*, but sadly it sank somewhere around this area a very long time ago."

"Do you know where the wreck is,
Captain Andy?" asked Thomas, one of
the boys on the trip.

Captain Andy shook his head. "We
don't know exactly where the ship sank,"
he replied. "It had a beautiful carved and
painted figure of a mermaid attached
to its front. The legend says that the
mermaid statue now watches over this
area from wherever the wreck lies on the
bed of the ocean."

"What a great story," Rachel remarked
to Kirsty. "It sounds like magic!"

"And we know all about *that*, don't
we Rachel?" Kirsty whispered, winking
at her friend.

The two girls were right in the middle
of another exciting, magical fairy
adventure.

When they'd arrived in Leamouth, they'd received an invitation to visit the Fairyland Ocean Gala, where they'd met their old friend Shannon the Ocean Fairy. Rachel and Kirsty had also been introduced to Shannon's helpers, the seven Ocean Fairies, and their Magical Ocean Creatures, who lived in the Royal Aquarium.

Shannon had explained to Rachel and Kirsty that the most important part of the Gala was when she played a tune on the Magical Golden Conch Shell. This would make sure that there was peace and harmony in all the oceans for the next year.

But just as Shannon was preparing to play her tune, Jack Frost and his goblin servants had barged in and disrupted the ceremony.

Jack Frost had ordered the goblins to steal the Golden Conch Shell, and they'd all rushed to grab it before the horrified fairies could stop them.

But as the goblins fought over which one of them should hold the shell, they'd dropped it, and, with a crash, it had shattered into seven jagged pieces.

Jack Frost had been furious at the goblins' clumsiness.

But, with a blast of icy magic from his wand, he'd immediately sent the shell fragments spinning through the air to hide themselves in different places throughout the human world.

Both Jack Frost and the fairies knew that without the Magical Golden Conch Shell, there would be chaos and confusion in the oceans.

However, Queen Titania had tried to limit the power of Jack Frost's spell by using her own magic to send the Ocean Fairies' seven Magical Ocean Creatures to find the shell pieces and guard them until they could be safely returned to Fairyland. Rachel and Kirsty were helping the Ocean Fairies in their quest, but they had to keep a sharp lookout for Jack Frost's goblins who were searching for the missing fragments of shell, too.

"I wonder if we'll find another piece of the Magical Golden Conch Shell today," Kirsty murmured to Rachel as they sailed further out to sea. "The shell's almost complete again, now. Only two more pieces left to find!"

"Don't forget the Fairy Queen says we have to wait for the magic to come to us,"

Rachel reminded her. "Let's just enjoy
the boat trip and see what happens!"

Suddenly Thomas
gave a cry.

"What's *that*?"
he shouted,
pointing at the
foamy waves
ahead of them.
"I can see
something moving."

"Use your binoculars, sailors!" Captain
Andy called. All the passengers had
been given a set of binoculars when they
boarded the *Ocean Star*, and now Rachel
and Kirsty peered through theirs eagerly.
At first they couldn't see anything much,
but then they both noticed some flashes
of movement on the horizon.

"Wow!" Captain Andy exclaimed, sounding very excited. "The *Mermaid* has certainly brought us good luck today. It's a school of whales!"

"Oh!" Rachel gasped with delight as she spotted a black and white whale surge up from beneath the waves and then splash down into the water again. "Oh, Kirsty, aren't they *beautiful*?"

"They're gorgeous!" Kirsty was breathless with excitement, her eyes glued to the binoculars. There were three whales surfacing now, blowing sparkling jets of water from their blowholes.

"They're killer whales," Captain Andy explained as everyone watched the whales in delight. "Killer whales belong to the dolphin family, and they often live in large family groups, called pods."

Just then, Kirsty noticed another, smaller whale leap out of the water behind the others. He blew a spurt of water from his blowhole, and Kirsty caught her breath as she noticed a faint glimmer of silver sparkles around the whale.

"Rachel, look!" Kirsty whispered, lowering her binoculars and turning to her friend. "That whale at the back is glowing with fairy magic. I think

it's one of the Magical Ocean Creatures
from the Royal Aquarium – and that
means a piece of the Magical Golden
Conch Shell is close by!"

Whales at Play

Her heart thumping with excitement,
Rachel stared through the binoculars
and spotted the whale's glittering tail just
before he dived below the waves again.

"You're right, Kirsty!" she said eagerly.
"He must be Whitney the Whale Fairy's
whale. I wonder if Whitney is somewhere
around here, too?"

"I'll steer the boat closer to the whales so we can all get a better look," Captain Andy called, turning the ship's wheel, and everyone cheered. Rachel and Kirsty waited impatiently as the ship slowly changed course and began to move towards the whales. The girls were worried that the whales might swim away before they reached them, but they seemed happy to frolic around in the ocean, blowing out jets of water, rolling over and flicking their tails to and fro.

The whales seemed to be calling to each other every so often, too, with strange, sweet sounds.

Suddenly a loud burst of noise interrupted the peace of the ocean. Rachel and Kirsty spun round and saw a speedboat zooming across the water in the direction of the whales.

"Oh no!" Rachel groaned, clapping her hands over her ears. "That noise is going to scare the whales away!"

Everyone on the *Ocean Star*, including
the girls, watched anxiously as the
speedboat headed straight towards
the whales. But
suddenly the
driver of the
boat slowed
down and
changed
his course,
beginning to
head away
from them.
"Thank
goodness!"
Kirsty sighed
with relief. "The
crew must have spotted the
whales at the last minute."

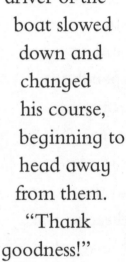

But then, to everyone's amazement, all the whales turned round and swam straight after the speedboat. Within a few seconds the whales were right behind the boat and then they moved up to swim alongside it.

"Well, that's very odd," Captain Andy said, looking surprised. "They don't seem bothered by the noise one bit!"

The whales were now splashing playfully around the boat, sending up sprays of water from their blowholes, and not looking scared at all.

"I think the speedboat is trying to get away from them," Rachel pointed out as the boat began to weave from side to side.

"They're not having much luck though," Kirsty replied. "Look, the whales are *still* following them."

Captain Andy was shaking his head in astonishment. "I've never seen whales behave this way before," he declared, looking very puzzled. "I just don't understand it."

Rachel and Kirsty glanced knowingly at each other.

"The whales are behaving strangely because the Magical Golden Conch Shell is broken," Rachel whispered to Kirsty. "Nothing will be right in the oceans until the Conch Shell is whole again, and Shannon can play it."

"Hello, girls!" called a tinkling, silvery voice. "I'm over here!"

Kirsty grabbed Rachel's arm. "Rachel, did you hear that?" she asked.

Rachel nodded. "I think it came from down there!" she said, pointing over the side of the *Ocean Star*.

Everyone else was still watching the whales, so Rachel and Kirsty slipped away unnoticed and peered over the side.

"Look, Kirsty!" Rachel exclaimed. She pointed down at a red-and-white striped buoy floating on the water near the ship, and Kirsty saw a tiny, glittering fairy perched on top of it.

"Hello, girls!" the fairy called again, waving at them. She had shiny black bobbed hair and she wore a floaty, strappy dress in deep shades of purple, yellow and red, with matching yellow ballet slippers.

"It's me, Whitney the Whale Fairy. I'm very worried about my whale, Flukey! I know you've seen him having a lovely time playing with the other whales and chasing after that speedboat."

Rachel and Kirsty nodded.

"The problem is that Flukey is following the boat further and further away from the part of the ocean where the shell piece is," Whitney went on anxiously. "We don't have much hope of finding the shell piece without Flukey's help, so we need to stop him! Will you help me, girls?"

Seaweed Surprise

"Of course we'll help!" Rachel and Kirsty said together.

Whitney looked very relieved.

"Is it safe for me to come on board?" she asked.

Kirsty took a quick look over her shoulder. Everyone else was standing with their backs to the girls, still watching the whales.

"It's quite safe,
Whitney," Kirsty
told her.

Whitney fluttered
upwards, her wings
dazzling in the bright
sunlight, and landed on the
ship's rail. "I'll turn you into
fairies, girls," she whispered,
lifting her wand. "Then we'll fly
after Flukey as fast as we can!"

Rachel and Kirsty saw a shower of
magical sparkles shoot from Whitney's
wand and surround them.

Instantly the girls felt themselves begin
to shrink down to fairy-size, as they'd
done so many times before, complete
with their own sets of glittering,
translucent wings.

"Let's go!" Whitney cried, swooping off the side of the ship. "If we keep just above the waves, the movement of our wings will be masked by the sunlight glinting off the water."

Kirsty and Rachel followed her, fluttering off the ship's rail and out across the ocean. Below them the white-tipped waves rolled and broke against the enormous wooden sides of the ship.

"The *Ocean Star* looks even bigger now we're fairy-sized!" Rachel called to Kirsty as they headed towards Flukey and the other whales.

The speedboat was continuing to circle
and weave its way through the water,
but it still hadn't managed to shake the
whales off.

"There's Flukey!" Whitney said, pointing
out the small whale with
the sparkly tail the
girls had noticed
earlier.

Flukey was
swimming happily
along behind the
speedboat with
another whale.

"Can you call him,
Whitney?" Kirsty asked.

Whitney frowned. "I'm not sure he'll
hear me above the noise of the boat,"
she replied. "Let's go a little closer."

As Whitney and the girls flew nearer
to the boat, Rachel noticed something
rather odd about the crew. They all
looked the same, with very long noses and
very large feet. And they were *green*…

"Goblins!" Rachel exclaimed, pointing
them out to Kirsty and Whitney.

"They must be looking for the shell
piece, too," Kirsty added.

"And the shell piece might be closer
than they think!" Whitney said in a
dismayed voice.
"Girls, look at
Flukey's tail. Can
you see what I
see?"

The girls stared
down at the little whale's tail as it
splashed in and out of the water.

They could see a clump of green seaweed caught on the end of it.

Then Rachel and Kirsty spotted a gleam of magical golden light in the middle of the seaweed.

"It's the missing shell piece!" Kirsty gasped, "It's tangled up in the seaweed on Flukey's tail!"

"Which means Flukey *isn't* swimming further away from the shell piece at all," Whitney pointed out. "In fact, he's taking the shell right to the goblins!"

"How can we stop him, Whitney?" Rachel asked urgently.

Below them, the group of goblins was looking very panicky as the whales continued to swim playfully around the boat. They were huddled together on the deck, unsure what to do.

"Go away, horrible fishy things!" the biggest goblin shouted. "We were only looking for the magic whale – we don't want to be chased by the whole lot of you!"

"Why won't they stop following us?" the smallest goblin squeaked nervously.

Suddenly all the whales, including Flukey, plunged down under the water out of sight. The goblins looked very relieved.

But a few seconds later the whales resurfaced with very loud splashes in different places. Now, instead of being just behind the boat, Flukey was swimming alongside it.

Then one of the goblins gave a yelp of triumph.

"I can see the missing piece of the

Golden Conch Shell!" he cried, his gaze
fixed on Flukey's tail.

"Flukey, dive under the water again!"
Whitney yelled, zooming down with
Rachel and Kirsty right behind her.

But it was too late. Flukey was so
surprised to hear
Whitney's voice,
he glanced
upwards,
giving the
goblins just
enough time
to lean over

the side of the boat and
untangle the shell piece from his tail.

"Got it!" the big goblin roared, waving
the shell in the air. "For once, we've got
the better of those pesky fairies!"

The goblin who'd spotted the shell scowled. "*I* saw it first!" he complained, "Give it to me!" And he tried to grab the shell from the big goblin.

"Get off!" the big goblin howled as they each pulled at the piece of shell like they were playing tug-of-war.

Suddenly, the gleaming golden shell slipped from their grasp. It sailed over the edge of the boat and landed with a splash in the ocean.

The two goblins turned to each other.

"Now look what you made me do!" they both said furiously, at exactly the same moment.

"It's the fairies' fault!" one of the other goblins yelled. "They're always interfering and making things go wrong!"

Whitney turned to Rachel and Kirsty

as the goblins began arguing over who
was to blame.

"While the goblins are grumbling and
complaining, we can dive into the ocean
to find the shell piece!" she said. "Are you
ready, girls?"

Shipwreck!

Rachel and Kirsty nodded excitedly.

"Let's go!" Rachel cried.

Whitney swished her wand above
the girls' heads and out of the mist of
fairy dust, two shiny, translucent bubbles
appeared in the air. The bubbles floated
gently downwards, and one settled over
Rachel's head, and the other over Kirsty's.

The girls weren't nervous at all, because this had happened to them several times before on their fairy adventures. They didn't even jump when the bubbles disappeared with a faint *pop*!

"And now you'll be able to breathe underwater," Whitney reminded them with a smile. "Down, down, down, we go!"

And she dived into the waves head-first, like a swimmer off a diving-board.

Rachel and Kirsty followed. They sank beneath the water and there they saw Flukey circling around waiting for them. He looked enormous to the girls now that they were fairy-sized as he rushed over to greet them.

"I'm sorry, Whitney," Flukey sang, looking a little dejected. "I didn't realise the shell piece was caught on my tail."

"Don't worry." Whitney patted Flukey's smooth dark head. "It must be around here *somewhere*. Let's start looking for it right away."

Whitney, Rachel, Kirsty and Flukey began to swim slowly along just below the surface of the water, searching for the missing fragment of shell. Shoals of pretty pink, blue and yellow fish stared at them curiously as they passed by.

Suddenly, Kirsty gave a startled shout. "Have you spotted the shell?" Rachel asked eagerly.

"No, but look at that octopus!" Kirsty said, pointing ahead of them. An octopus was floating through the water upside-down, waving its eight legs gracefully above its head.

"And see those fish over there?" Kirsty went on. "Aren't they funny?"

"They're catfish," Whitney explained as the girls stared at the rather strange-looking fish with their large eyes and whiskery mouths. As they watched, one of the catfish chased after a length of driftwood floating in the water. He grabbed it in his teeth and took it back to the others.

Rachel and Kirsty couldn't believe what they were seeing!

"Catfish?" Rachel said with a grin. "They're more like *dogfish*!"

"Whitney, is this strange behaviour all because of the Golden Conch Shell?" Kirsty asked.

Whitney nodded, her face serious. "This kind of chaos is going on all over the oceans," she said. "We *have* to find that missing piece before the goblins do!"

Suddenly Flukey gave a squeak of warning. "Humans!" he sang, pointing a flipper up to the surface. There, spot lit by the bright sunshine above the ocean, were five dark shapes, swimming along very fast towards them.

"We need to hide, and quickly!" Whitney declared. "Let's go deeper into the ocean, girls. Hurry!"

Whitney, Rachel, Kirsty and Flukey swam as fast as they could towards the ocean floor. It got darker the deeper they went, but then Rachel spotted something.

"There's a big black shape at the very bottom of the ocean just below us," she told the others. "Maybe we can hide inside it."

They all headed towards it. As they got closer, Kirsty turned to Rachel.

"I think it's a shipwreck!" she declared.

Kirsty was right. The enormous, wooden hull of an old-fashioned sailing ship like the *Ocean Star* lay on the sandy ocean floor. The masts had broken in half and the timbers were rotting away, while brightly coloured fish floated lazily in and out of the portholes.

"The ship looks very old," Rachel observed as they swam closer.

"I wonder if it could be the *Mermaid* that Captain Andy told us about?"

A splashing sound behind them made everyone jump.

"The swimmers are catching up with us," Whitney said. "Hide!"

Flukey zoomed around to the other side of the ship and hid behind a large rock. Meanwhile, Whitney, Rachel and Kirsty swam through a large hole in the ship's deck and found themselves in a cabin full of water.

There was nothing in the cabin except a large wooden chest bobbing around.

Then they heard voices above them. Whitney put a finger to her lips and they peeped out of the hole they'd just swum through.

Five figures were
heading towards the
shipwreck. As they
hovered above the
deck, Rachel could
see that they had clear
bubbles over their
heads and flippers
on their feet.

"They're not
humans," she whispered. "They're the
goblins from the speedboat!"

"We must find the shell piece before
they do," Whitney said in a low voice.
"But be careful, girls!"

Silently, the three friends swam out of
the cabin and began to search the rest of
the ship. The goblins didn't notice. They

were swimming across to the other end of the deck, towards the ship's wheel.

"The captain always stands *here*," the big goblin said importantly, grasping the wheel.

"And as I'm bigger than all of you, *I'll* be the captain."

"Yes, you're the biggest," agreed one of the goblins, "But you're also the *silliest*! I'll be captain. I'm extremely clever!"

"Well, if you're so clever, what's *that* for, then?" asked the smallest goblin, pointing at the ship's wheel.

The second goblin looked a little sheepish. "I don't know," he confessed.

As the goblins bickered, Whitney and the girls split up and carefully searched the ship for the missing fragment of shell. Rachel began poking around the rotting timbers of one of the ship's masts which lay on the deck.

But as she peeked gently underneath a piece of mast, the old wood crumbled at her touch and fell to bits. Rachel was taken completely by surprise and gave a loud gasp.

Immediately all the goblins spun round.

"It's one of those pesky fairies!" the big goblin yelled. "She can show us where the shell piece is. Grab her!"

Treasure Trove

On the other side of the ship, Whitney and Kirsty had heard all this. Now they stared at each other in horror.

"The goblins are going to capture Rachel!" Whitney whispered. "We have to stop them!"

Kirsty glanced around desperately for inspiration. Then she spotted the hole in the deck where they'd hidden earlier.

"I have an idea," Kirsty announced. "Quick, Whitney, back to the cabin!"

They swam across to the gap in the wooden timbers and slipped down the hole into the water-filled cabin again. The wooden chest was still floating around the room, its lid half-open. Kirsty went over to peep inside.

"Whatever was in here has rotted away," she told Whitney. "It's full of seashells and seaweed now. Brilliant!"

Whitney looked confused. "How is that going to help Rachel?" she asked.

"This looks like a treasure chest, right?" Kirsty replied with a grin. "And with a little fairy magic, maybe we can make the seashells and seaweed look like treasure, too, so that we can distract the goblins!"

"What a great idea!" Whitney laughed, and with one wave of her wand, she sent a shower of sparkles raining down on the wooden chest. Kirsty grinned as the shells and seaweed were transformed into shining golden crowns and long necklaces of glittering emeralds, rubies, sapphires and diamonds.

"Let's hope this works," Whitney whispered to Kirsty as they flew back to the deck. "I don't know how long my magic will last."

Outside, Rachel was darting around, trying desperately to escape from the goblin's clutches.

"Hey, Rachel!" Kirsty called loudly. "Forget about that silly shell piece. We've found something even better in this cabin – a chest full of treasure!"

All the goblins whirled round.

"TREASURE!" they roared excitedly. "Hurrah!"

And, losing all interest in Rachel, the goblins swam speedily across the deck and down into the cabin.

"Are you all right, Rachel?" Whitney called as she hurried to join her. Rachel nodded gratefully. Meanwhile, Kirsty was peeping through the hole in the deck at the goblins in the cabin below.

"The goblins are draping themselves in the necklaces and wearing the crowns on their heads!" Kirsty laughed.

"Well, the goblins are out of the way for the moment," Whitney said. "But we've searched everywhere and we *still* haven't found the shell."

"Maybe Flukey can help," Rachel suggested.

"Flukey!" Whitney called. "Where are you?"

"Over here," Flukey sang out a reply. He'd swum out from behind the rock and was now hovering near the prow of the shipwreck, which was covered in large clumps of seaweed. Whitney and the girls swam over to him.

"There's something hidden under the seaweed," Flukey told Whitney excitedly.

Rachel, Kirsty and Whitney pulled the feathery green fronds aside. And underneath, attached to the prow of the ship, they saw a carved wooden figure of a mermaid with long flowing hair and a fish's tail.

"So this shipwreck is the *Mermaid* after all!" Kirsty exclaimed.

"She's lovely," Rachel sighed, gazing at the mermaid's beautiful, serene face.

Kirsty nodded, then gave a cry of surprise. "Look at the mermaid's hair!" she gasped.

Whitney, Rachel and Flukey stared closely. Nestling in the mermaid's long flowing locks, like a golden hair comb, was the missing shell piece!

But just as Rachel reached out her hand to grab it, the goblins swam up onto the deck. They had strands of seaweed around their necks and large shells on their heads, and they looked *very* cross and *very* silly.

"My magic has worn off!" Whitney whispered.

"Look, there's the shell piece!" the big goblin yelled, pulling the seaweed off his neck. "Let's grab it!"

Goblin Fountains!

"Quick, Flukey!" Whitney said, as the goblins began to swim towards them. "We need your help!"

Flukey nodded. He opened his mouth and a beautiful, sweet, whale song poured out, echoing throughout the depths of the ocean. Rachel and Kirsty had never heard anything quite so amazing.

Suddenly, there was an answering call in the distance. A few moments later, the girls gasped as the other whales came diving down through the water towards them very fast. The goblins' eyes almost popped out of their heads when they saw the enormous whales heading in their direction. "Let's get out of here!" they yelled. And forgetting all about the shell, they turned and began to swim away as speedily as they could.

But the whales were quicker. Five of them swam up behind the goblins and each whale scooped up one of the goblins gently with their nose, tipping them onto their backs. All the goblins shrieked with fear as the whales then headed back up to the surface of the ocean, taking the goblins with them.

"Let us go, horrible fishy things!" the smallest goblin yelped.

Immediately, Rachel grabbed the shell piece from the mermaid's hair.

"Thank you," she whispered to the carved figure.

"Grab onto Flukey's tail, girls, and we'll follow the other whales!" Whitney told them.

The girls did as she said. Flukey went zooming upwards, back towards the surface of the ocean, pulling Whitney, Kirsty and Rachel easily behind him. As they broke through the waves into the sunlight again, they all burst out laughing at the scene in front of them.

The whales that had picked up the goblins were shooting tall fountains from their blowholes, and the goblins were bouncing around on top of the huge jets of water, unable to escape. The goblins looked extremely cross.

"Let me go!" one of them was shouting, "I don't want to be a goblin fountain!"

Meanwhile, the other whales were swimming around them, performing graceful flips, turns and rolls in the water. It was a magical sight.

Whitney turned to Rachel and Kirsty.

"I don't think the goblins are going to bother us again for a little while!" she said. "Time to take you back to the *Ocean Star*, girls."

Immediately Flukey shrank down to his fairy-size. Whitney tucked the whale firmly under her arm and then, with another flick of her wrist, her magic whisked them all back to the deck of the *Ocean Star*.

Luckily, Captain Andy and everyone else on board were still at the other end of the deck, and didn't notice a thing. Then Whitney quickly used her magical fairy dust to make Rachel and Kirsty their normal size again.

"Oh, that was a fantastic fairy adventure!" Kirsty sighed happily. "I'm so glad we found the shell piece."

"And now there's only one piece left to find before the Magical Golden Conch Shell is whole again," Rachel added.

"Thank you so much, girls," Whitney said. "Flukey and I couldn't have done it without you. And now we must take the shell back to Fairyland. Shannon and the other Ocean Fairies are going to be thrilled!"

Rachel and Kirsty gave Flukey a

goodbye pat, and then waved as Whitney and her whale disappeared in a flurry of glittering sparkles.

"Rachel! Kirsty!" Thomas came running towards the girls, looking very excited.

"The whales are back! They disappeared for a little while, but now they're here again. Aren't we lucky to see them?"

"Yes," Kirsty replied, exchanging a secret smile with Rachel. "We're very lucky indeed!"

Now it's time for Kirsty and Rachel to help...

Courtney the Clownfish Fairy

Read on for a sneak peek...

"I can't believe we're going home tomorrow," Rachel Walker said, gazing out to sea. "This has been *such* a brilliant holiday!"

"I know," her best friend Kirsty Tate agreed. "I'll never forget it."

The two girls were standing on the end of Leamouth Pier, leaning against the railings. It was a warm, clear day, and the sun cast dancing sparkles on the water below. Jolly music boomed out from the funfair behind them. Kirsty and Rachel had been staying with Kirsty's gran for a week of the spring holiday, and it had been a very exciting time. They had met the seven Ocean Fairies, and enjoyed some wonderful adventures with them, trying to find the lost pieces of a Magical Golden Conch Shell.

Rachel sighed. "I'm a bit worried, you know. We still haven't found the last piece of the Conch Shell, and time's running out."

"We can't let the holiday end without finding it," Kirsty replied. "I really hope we meet Courtney the Clownfish Fairy soon!"

Kirsty and Rachel had met the Ocean Fairies on the first day of their holiday, when they'd been invited to a special Ocean Gala Party in Fairyland.

Every year at the party, Shannon

the Ocean Fairy played a song on the Magical Golden Conch Shell, which would ensure happy times in and around the ocean for everyone. But this year, before she could play the tune, mean Jack Frost had gatecrashed the party, sneering that he hated the seaside. He didn't like seeing anyone enjoy themselves and loathed getting sand between his toes! He'd ordered his goblin servants to seize the Golden Conch Shell, but unfortunately they'd started squabbling over it, then dropped it...

Read Courtney the Clownfish Fairy to find out what adventures are in store for Kirsty and Rachel!

Meet the
Ocean Fairies

**Naughty goblins have smashed the magical conch
shell! Kirsty and Rachel must restore it
so that the oceans can have harmony again.**

www.rainbowmagicbooks.co.uk

Win Rainbow Magic Goodies!

There are lots of Rainbow Magic fairies, and we want to know which one is your favourite! Send us a picture of her and tell us in thirty words why she is your favourite and why you like Rainbow Magic books. Each month we will put the entries into a draw and select one winner to receive a Rainbow Magic Sparkly T-shirt and Goody Bag!

Send your entry on a postcard to Rainbow Magic Competition, Orchard Books, 338 Euston Road, London NW1 3BH.
Australian readers should email: childrens.books@hachette.com.au
New Zealand readers should write to Rainbow Magic Competition, PO Box 3255, Shortland St, Auckland 1140, NZ.
Don't forget to include your name and address.
Only one entry per child.

Good luck!

Meet the
Friendship Fairies

When Jack Frost steals the Friendship Fairies' magical objects, BFFs everywhere are in trouble! Can Rachel and Kirsty help save the magic of friendship?

www.rainbowmagicbooks.co.uk

The Rainbow Magic Reading Challenge

Well done, fairy friend – you have completed the book!
This book was worth 5 points.

See how far you have climbed on the
Reading Rainbow opposite.

The more books you read, the more points you will get,
and the closer you will be to becoming a Fairy Princess!

How to get your Reading Rainbow
1. Cut out the coin below
2. Go to the Rainbow Magic website
3. Download and print out your poster
4. Add your coin and climb up the Reading Rainbow!

There's all this and lots more at
www.rainbowmagicbooks.co.uk

You'll find activities, competitions, stories, a special
newsletter and complete profiles of all the
Rainbow Magic fairies. Find a fairy with your name!